cemetery miss you

Jason S Polley

Proverse Hong Kong

cemetery miss you recounts the first year or so of a Pakistani illegal's experiences in Hong Kong. The work begins by detailing the boy-man's middle-class experiences in Pakistan, before he's all-but-forced to flee the place after shooting a man severally point-blank in the name of family honour. His life in Hong Kong begins as a life of poverty, living on the streets. Less than a year later he's buying rounds of drinks on The Peak, driving around in private cars, spending thousands of dollars on footwear, and making regular short trips to mainland China.

Saa Ji, a name adopted by a host of Indian Subcontinent illegals and refugees in Hong Kong, tells not only his own story, but also the untold story of so many peripheral figures in Hong Kong, figures compelled into unimaginably intricate underworld networks—and not because of ethical unsoundness or suspectness. Instead, these perpetually marginalized and institutionally desperate figures have no other options. Saa Ji speaks of alterity in Hong Kong, of the otherness we all criminally ignore.

Jason S Polley divides his time between reading, scuba diving, practicing yoga, motorcycling, and getting tattooed. His first book, a collection of short travel narratives in verse, titled "refrain", was published by Proverse in 2010. "cemetery miss you" captures the memoirs of a man who categorically goes by the anonymous moniker "Saa Ji," as do a litany of Hong Kong's Pakistani and Indian illegal residents. "cemetery miss you" was begun in May 2009 and completed one-year later so as to meet the deadline for the 2010 Proverse Prize. Since 1998, Polley has lived in Guangzhou, Montreal, Bogota, Guayaquil, and Hong Kong. He's currently assistant professor of literary theory, American culture, and contemporary fiction at Hong Kong Baptist University.

cemetery miss you

"When you feel the big shiver through body, and for no reason, it's because the cemetery miss you." — Saa Ji

Jason S Polley

Proverse Hong Kong

cemetery miss you
by Jason S Polley.
2nd pbk edition published in Hong Kong by Proverse Hong Kong
ISBN: 978-988-8228-47-8
Copyright © Proverse Hong Kong, May 2016.

1st published in pbk in Hong Kong by Proverse Hong Kong, 22 November 2011.
Copyright © Proverse Hong Kong, 22 November 2011.
ISBN 978-988-19932-8-1

Enquiries: Proverse Hong Kong, P. O. Box 259, Tung Chung Post Office, Tung Chung,
Lantau, NT, Hong Kong SAR, China.
E-mail: proverse@netvigator.com Web site: www.proversepublishing.com

The right of Jason S Polley to be identified as the author of this work has been asserted
by him in accordance with the Copyright, Designs and Patents Act 1988. The right of Ina
Grigorova to be identified as the author of "Preface" has been asserted by her in
accordance with the Copyright, Designs and Patents Act 1988.

Cover design by Artist Hong Kong Company,Unit D3, G/F, Phase 3, Kwun Tong
Industrial Centre, 448-458 Kwun Tong Road, Kowloon, Hong Kong.

Front cover image by Jason S Polley
Back cover image by Maria Fernada Jaramillo Zapata.

1st edition CIP Block
Proverse Hong Kong

British Library Cataloguing in Publication Data

Polley, Jason S.
cemetery miss you.
1. Pakistanis--China--Hong Kong--Fiction. 2. Illegal
aliens--China--Hong Kong--Fiction. 3. Hong Kong
(China)--Social conditions--Fiction.
I. Title
813.6-dc23

ISBN-13: 9789881993281

Souls cross ages likes clouds cross skies, an' tho' a cloud's shape nor hue nor size don't stay the same, it's still a cloud an' so is a soul. Who can say where the cloud's blowed from or who'll the soul'll be 'morrow? Only [God] the east an' the west an' the compass and the atlas, yay, only the atlas o' clouds.

Cloud Atlas, David Mitchell

Preface

Catalino is so smooth and eloquent in his natural habitat—language—that it almost makes sense he had to write this book in order to meet Saa Ji, who seems to be his cosmic antiparticle. And it makes sense that the fugitive-turned-moods-supplier Saa Ji would choose Catalino to confide in.

Who would want to tell the story of his life to someone who could have lived it?

I happened to be in Hong Kong while Catalino was recording these files; I was even lucky enough to meet the protagonist. The meeting was not entirely pleasant, but Saa Ji was pretty damn real. (I hereby certify that Catalino did not make Saa Ji up.)

But what I find most compelling about this story: Catalino didn't even get to translate it. Saa Ji did. And in that very act Saa Ji created himself.

As a linguist and an ex-pat who writes in her third language, I think about translation a lot. To twist Rodriguez' famous punch line from *Machete*: "When we cross the border, the border crosses us"—and we begin to re-package ourselves into pieces that can be smuggled across the internalized border of our new language. In that process we not only rebuild ourselves, we also rebuild the world. That's the lowdown of linguistic relativity for you. But bear with me.

I was visiting Hong Kong to work on a Science Fiction novel. My idea of a fun read was to mess with the reader's perception of time, to make the effect cause the cause, to watch language create what it speaks…the whole deal.

The setting for my Saa Ji encounter was a small car-free Hong Kong island away from the skyscrapers. Nature was exploding at the seams to prove a point. I was standing to the side as Catalino and Saa Ji spoke and *transacted*. I was trying not to impose, but I wasn't going out of my way to be invisible. It was a lovely day's end, giant spiders were weaving their webs, the frangipani were blooming. So I felt I should do some power yoga to, you know, blend with it all. To *imprint*. The pose I chose was not, to my western gestalt, especially provocative or unladylike, but it was an advanced pose, one that still tends to evoke an "OMG you can do that?" response.

I think Saa Ji was sick that day and not in the best of moods (I had offered him some natural stuff for his throat, which he declined). Still, I was blown away when he turned to me and said, as dispassionately as if he was telling me yoga was fine but he himself preferred Tai Chi, "In my country, they will kill you with stones if you do this."

I was not expecting that. The comment made my vision vibrate. It was also my birthday—which probably explains what I was doing at the event horizon of said "age-of-resin" transaction. Birthdays are not my thing; even as a kid, I always felt somehow grandly mistreated by the universe on that day.

Catalino and I left soon after that.

He tried to apologize for Saa Ji later. He mentioned he was recording the man's story. I appreciated the effort to distract me by way of the literary value of the experience. But there was, in retrospect, nothing to apologize for—or too much to even start.

To be fair, there had been no anger in Saa Ji's voice. Immersed in his story and distracted by me, he had probably glimpsed the worlds (the one he had left and the one he was now inhabiting). The two were lined up split-frame in front of him, and he was just reporting the obvious break in the symmetry. For all I know, his dispassion was a compliment. Or dismay that people could think of throwing stones on a planet that smelled so much like flowers.

Or maybe I'm just that annoying when I'm waiting to get stoned.

Imagine my surprise when, a couple of years later, I got a note from Catalino, saying, amongst other things, "I know you were made basically nauseated by the man—that's why you need to preface his story. It will hook you; and then it all falls apart, like all things, but this so vastly sadly…"

So I sat and read, after months of resistance, the story of this man who'd made me realize with chilled bones that there are places on earth where the known laws of social physics simply fall apart.

A stooped posture, a cough, waves of wary curiosity, then he'd remember there is safety in indifference. I can almost reconstruct Saa Ji from the re-packaged fragments of self he himself smuggled out. Catalino's snapshot animation of this process is like inspecting an open watch not just tick but actually melt and reassemble itself to show the new hour as it crosses a time zone. Catalino's is a text with the wheels of its own cognitive process both at work and exposed.

As a builder of alien worlds, I was prime target for *cemetery miss you*'s charms. The people and events in the story are grainy, pixelated, blinking on and off; reality has been exposed at the Planck scale where any apparent continuity breaks down. Hong Kong is a good substrate for Sci-Fi constructs, not just because HK is so insanely futuristic, a spread-out tower of Babel, and not just because if you squint you can picture *cemetery*'s characters crossing states more exotic than national boundaries (while borrowing each other's passports and pasts), but also because the book's very surface approaches quantum foam: objects of characterization blinking on and off, end-positioned subjects slipping away into the next sentence predicate; cause and effect inverting, like the thought-wave must flow in Saa Ji's native-tongue state. His language starts with adverbials (when, how, why), and after some excursions of uncertainty ends with the concrete who and what, thus upholding the superposition of all possible outcomes much longer than fluent English ever could. I had been killed with a Schroedinger's stone, *both* a compliment and a curse, by a man simultaneously innocent and guilty—at once a fugitive and always-already at home, hating and loving his new self and life, proud and ashamed, "halal and haram." To the end Saa Ji can't figure out why it feels so not right to be him. It is that last part which brings it home, even to a reader fluent, eloquent and legal, who could have never lived the life of Saa Ji. The final part that falls apart.

Maybe when one of us crosses the border, we all cross the border—because with all the splitting of selves, with this windfall of change, the opposite has to be true. This, to preserve the symmetry, if nothing else.

No one is only one person.

Yet, in all this coming and going, we are all of us the same person trying to stay the same.

Ina Grigorova
New York

For Krista, for Catalina.

And Aadab, and Abdul-ji.

Author's Introduction

After a characteristically interminable-seeming 18-hour flight to Hong Kong from Montreal, via Ottawa and Chicago, I boarded an express train followed by two ferries and finally made my weary way to a cousin's place in a remote village on Lamma Island. My sweat yet-dry, a knock came upon the door. I unlatched it to a mumbled Hi, I'm Saa Ji as a flaming black-smoke-billowing hand-rolled cigarette was pressed into my half-open hand. Welcome to Lamma, the black apparition offered as it disappeared way faster than the ghost of Hamlet's father.

And so began my at-first dubious then noteworthy friendship with the remarkable yet by no means distinct (in Hong Kong at least) antihero of *cemetery miss you*. Always under cover of darkness, Saa Ji and I would randomly cross paths every fortnight or so. He always produced the same stimulating Age of Reason gift. I soon learned always to have a tin of Tsing Tao beer (he dislikes red wine) in my backpack in polite exchange. It did not take long, however, for me to realize that his words were the real gift. Both in content and form, his sometimes bombastic, sometimes hyperbolic, stories coupled with their always captivating cadence were my true addiction. He came to the same realization. Unlike the majority of his putative "friends," who ranged from occidental professionals to south-asian labourers to local construction foremen, I liked to listen to him, not just procure something from him only to avoid him.

So his stories became more candid. And more incredible. They were desperate; yet also hopeful. I couldn't help but be reminded of Driss ben Hamed Charhadi's *A Life Full of Holes* (Grove Press, 1964), which details the hand-to-mouth survival of a kif (marijuana) selling youth in North Africa. The late (last of the Beats) Paul Bowles tape-recorded the memoir of the illiterate Moghrebi-speaking Charhadi in a few sittings. With little editorial intervention, Bowles translated the novel-tape to English. I decided to do something similar with Saa Ji's nonfictional narrative, only without translation. I would record his story, and then transcribe it, with the generous help of my sister, Krista, directly using his own words, his own international English, adopting creative license only in terms of form in order best to capture his own half-painful, half-celebratory hesitation and reflection.

cemetery miss you recounts the first year or so of a Pakistani illegal's experiences in Hong Kong. The work begins by detailing the boy-man's middle-class experiences in Pakistan, before he's all-but-forced to flee the place after shooting a man severally at point-blank range in the name of family honour. Thinking he's on his way to South Korea, the 17-year old arrives in Hong Kong with basically no money and basically no English. He's forced to sell his passport; forced to wander the streets barefoot; forced to eat scraps from the garbage; forced to sleep on Tsim Sha Tsui's star ferry, with only a newspaper for warmth.

Less than a year later he's buying rounds of drinks on The Peak, dating numerous Indonesian and Filipina domestic helpers, driving around in a private car, spending thousands of dollars on footwear, and making regular short "business" trips to mainland China. Saa Ji, a name adopted by a host of Indian Subcontinent illegals and refugees in Hong Kong, tells not only his own story, but also the untold story of so many peripheral figures in Hong Kong, figures compelled into unimaginably intricate underworld networks—and not because of ethical unsoundness or suspectness. Instead, these perpetually marginalized and institutionally desperate figures have no other options. Saa Ji speaks of alterity in Hong Kong, of the otherness we all criminally ignore.

The story does not end in epiphany. The underground lifestyle Saa Ji adopts—for family, for respect—leads, predictably, but, still, no less sadly, to yet another life full of holes. The narrative falls apart as Saa Ji tells it, as only *this* Saa Ji can tell it.

Jason S Polley
Writing as *Catalino Catalino*

Table of Contents

Preface by Ina Grigorova
Author's Introduction

folder b file 1: 0 min 17 sec	1
folder b file 2: 1 hr 7 min 13 sec	1
folder b file 5: 52 min 18 sec	53
from folder b file 6: 3 min 35 sec	111
from folder b file 8: 4 min 14 sec	114
from folder b file 9: 12 min 14 sec	114
from folder b file 10: 1 min 32 sec	114
from folder b file 13: 3 min 8 sec	114
from folder b file 14: 0 min 20 sec	114
from folder b file 15: 5 min 30 sec	114
fragments from folder b file 16: 17 min 34 sec	115
fragments from folder b file 17: 17 min 9 sec	115
from folder b file 28: 1 min 36 sec	116
from folder b file 32: 6 min 54 sec	116

Cover images
Front cover image:Pakistani meal prepared by Saa Ji.
Back cover background image: Figure in front of the Taj Mahal, India.

folder b file 1: 0 min 17 sec

hash

it come in sheet with a stamp
every sheet have to be stamp with a company name so

you always want the company name |

its valuable

you get the stamp on top
you pay the money for that

folder b file 2: 1 hr 7 min 13 sec

my name is saajid
i born in pakistan 1983
15 june

my father name tawfeek
my mother name aadab
i live in sialkot
punjab

born in muslim family
very nice people
|

4 uncles have
4 aunties
grandfather
grandmothers

then 2 brother have
2 sister

before we live together
with the grandfather
and uncles

and aunties

my uncle got married
aunties got married
got separate house

live with grandfather
grandmothers
mother
father
other brother and sisters

i go to nice school
pray every day

wake up early in morning
pray

go to mosque
go to school

mom make a breakfast
come back
go private tutor every day
every day

every day you have a hard work
morning you wake up
you go to mosque
go to school
come back from the school

change your clothe
get your lunch
go back to teacher
study from the school

go back 5 oclock
do your homework
sleep

cemetery miss you 2

from 1 class
2 grade
3 4 5 grade
7 8 9 grade
you have same routine every single day

i read holy quran 11 time
i read holy quran
read holy quran 11 time in mosque

and my brother is learn quran
without seeing he can read quran
the two brother can do it
and my sister still studying now

i study in the private school
my father pay a lot of money

not very nice

but in the english middle school
after middle school
i go in the government schools

my father got good business
with my grandfather
after that he start the showrooms

showroom selling the motorbike

business last
10 years ago
8 years ago
10 years ago he had that business

middle school
i didnt understand much

high school if i finish i get bicycle

cemetery miss you 3

got my small room for me
my brothers sleep with me

but in the day i got my room
i always stay there

not much to do

5 time i pray
my mom force me
my mom not there
no need to pray

not do much

for fun play cricket
fly kites

my mom dont like it
always tell me Dont fly the kites
because homework
wasting time
wasting money

in the roof always and
getting fight with the kids
flying the kite and abusing each and
the screaming in the roof

because you know
pakistan got small house
neighbourhood with walls
and always screaming

and you always have exam in the basant
in the festival of the kite so
you always making the kites during exams
at 13 14 15

and every year kite festival come

cemetery miss you 4

february march

your exams come
february march

so every year
you have same situation

so in high school
i go to government school

there i learn to smoke cigaret
skip the school
play the video game

in my class
its like 3 4 this 1 so

in the whole school
its like 30 student
50 student in whole school

but its alright because
government school

you pay no fees
so you learn nothing

because private school
after middle school
quite expensive
number 1 and number 2

even you study the private or government school
you still have to give the government board exams

actually i get love when im in 7 grade

she my neighbour
she the daughter of my mosque teacher

cemetery miss you 5

my imam

my imam is my morning time teacher in the mosque and
my imam is my school teacher and
my imam is my private teacher

every day 1 hour after school
so i get closer and closer to my girlfriend
every day so

her name is faatina

it make a big big problem in my family
neighbours and girls and boys Love things
screaming things

and my uncle getting fucked very crazy
everybody asking me lot of question

and of course i respect him
but asking him same question back

Of course you love her
But what about you

and man and mom beating me up

dad not
but mom beating me up

Why you doing this 1
Why you doing that 1

in that year im 7 8 class

grow up
you know
start to smoke cigaret

every month getting 300 rupees from my father

cemetery miss you 6

now my own bike
small room
play music

i have best friend
my neighbour
his name zuhayr
he know hes very handsome

my father
my parent
dont want i take time with him

because he work
he work in the factory

and i study

hes same as my age
we are very good friend

we smoke together and
i can cry in front of him
he can cry in front of me

in my neighbourhood not much people
not young as my age

its 3 4 year all bigger
or they all smaller so

i got my neighbour zuhayr
and i got 1 more zaahid

we are 3

in the school i have the friend
but not much good friend

i live far from the school

so friend dont come very much at home

always go out eat tobacco paan

Why you have to
Why you need enjoyment in there

eat tobacco pan
smoke cigaret and
that is it

drink coke

and nobody like we hang around in the streets

kid in the streets
in the night time

and hang around in the night time
outside in the street

that always happy

and that is what we do

no video games
no fucking
this kind of stuff

you know
pray

every year have lot of holy festivals come

all the friend together
always pray
serious serious

pray for few years

cemetery miss you 8

everybody pray
some people have to be force to pray

but pray seriously
from the heart

sometimes he wants to watch tv
man
he dont want to go

when you want to pray
you got a way

i got imam saalih
i get up early in the morning

early in the morning pray
in the speaker
5 time a day
sometime 4 time

have to write down with tick mark
today i give azan

Alahu akbar Alahu akbar Alahu akbar Alahu akbar

so i pray in the morning in the speaker
so i pray sometime 1 time
sometime 2 time 3 time
so all the kid getting together
Its my turn
My turn
My turn

im smoking cigaret
but very little
for fun

you dont need it
you just smoking

cemetery miss you 9

just for fun

youre not addicted
you dont need

youre not going to spend money for that
because you dont have money

you only get very little rupee a day and
you need to survive on that

you cant buy pepsi coke

you get some snacks

yes
ok
you can get chocolate but

you cant get coke that time

we live in the side part of pakistan
big city
close to jammu kashmir

we have summer hot
winter flooding
lot of rain
in government school
im getting farther and farther from
doing mosque and prayer but

mother is forcing and forcing but
not much time in the morning

and after 2 year i live in my auntie house
my 9 class
my 10 class

exam coming very heavy

cemetery miss you 10

i live with them
because they have ba and ma
my cousins and
they want to give me study and

they tell my father
No
Send him here
I want to tell him how To read it

they give me house and room and good

from there i start to learn the music liking and
things and
there i fall in love 1 more girl

her name is kamala

she is the same age as me and
very far relative of me and

i am very good friend with my cousin raatib

i can share with him everything i do
whatever i can talk to him

i can talk sex
cigarets
whatever i do

and hes a teacher
he have a school now

he study for his own self
run the house and make his own life

he dont smoke
dont do anything

dont drink
dont do anything and

everybody in the family want me to do like him

everybody telling me Be like him because
hes the nicest guy

so i stay 2 year with him
9 class and 10 class

you dont have the girls in the school
man

separate

mens school
girls school

if you need to meet the girls
man
you just see the girls

if you have a girlfriend
you just see her

you pick up her time
date you dont date
you pick up her time

you know time she go to school
you know time you going to see her

dont talk to her
just see her

very difficult to talk to her

girls dont have private mobile numbers so

cemetery miss you 12

if you want to talk to her
you have to call her house

somebody answer the phone you cant talk

you only have to talk to her
you have to guess if shes talking

not her mom
not her sister

so very difficult

its like talk with a girlfriend is a big thing
big deal

i pick up the time but
this is normal thing

you can pick up the neighbours but
stranger girls
other neighbourhood girls
youre going to make her time

always happen
and they are going to tell their brothers

and he just going to look at you

1 time
2 time
3 time
she tell the brother or

the brother watching you watching her
until the girl not going to be talk
nothing going to be happen

girl said already 1 thing
you cant do anything else

they will kill you
man

they not kill you
they going to talk to your parents
have a big drama for disturbing her

if you do the harassment then you are fucked
even the police cannot look or touch the girl

1 man
he walking his lady in body scarf

in burkha

the police coming and
they search him for drugs or

gun or
whatever

and then they looking the girl and

the man saying
Dont touch her
She my sister

but the police they searching her so
touching her everywhere so

the man
hes going home
putting the sister to bed and everything
getting the gun and
going to the three policemans and
shooting them

then hes going to the police station
put down the gun and

saying I did it
Because they done this 1

in 48 hours pakistan government leave him

security of you and
your respect

you can fight

i have 3 guns in my house

1 my grandfather buy for my father
1 my father buy for me
ak 47
1 i buy for my brother
shotgun

documents for everything

we use in the celebration

when i go back to pakistan i use in celebrations
i shot 48 cartridge

everybody use

kids play with fun
man

everybody have guns

its like a joke in there
everybody have

my father dont have the car
he have the bike

he promise me the bike if i start the college
but im failing the exam

after studying at my uncles

so i doing private tutor

1 year im studying at home and
this i got passed

but im failing in 1 thing
english

so my father said Son do it
Youre so close to getting your bike

Starting your college
Do it

but i said I not studying anymore
I dont want do it

i got a little bit sick in the pakistan

the doctor say
he say my mind my body not good circulation so

13 months in lahore doctor taking care of me

army doctor and
my father paying a lot of money

every 2 week month i have to go there and
my mother crying
so giving me the medicines

i having problem when i sit down i fall down and
something coming out from the mouth

it not spit
not foam
water coming out from the mouth so

cemetery miss you 16

going many places to see and
doctor

when i stand i drop
but when i sleep im not drop

so what he going to do
he make me sleep so

every day
day and night
i doze

he give me those pills
i sleep

after 13 month i ok so

after last time with doctor
my father going to doctors house with
sweets
clothe

have respect
he thank very much

2 time in my life i see my father cry
when his dad die and
when he have to bring me lahore

2 times i see my father cry in my life

he not cry
strongest man ever

i live in my auntie house
of course my father is not telling how i do
my auntie tell me

my father father having 2 wife

when my father only 6 month his mother die so
2nd mother not caring him

he have glasses
he not going to school

so at 6 year he going karachi and

he working
he lifting the heavy things

6 years old
he go karachi and
lifting the heavy things on his head

my father

my father

he run away from the house because
the torturing of the mom but

we having the people
the visitors
the festivals in the house when im 6 7

only we having because my father
he struggling a lot but

when 22 he starting with my grandfather
starting with the shop

he stay with my grandfather until 30 40 years

do the business
my father is a hard worker
man

just do for children
he never see anything

cemetery miss you 18

go anywhere

just only for children

he saying You want to study
What you want
You study london
What you want
I will borrow

Everything

my sisters 10 11
they are baby dolls
they are running everywhere
everything

but 12 13 year old
they are wearing scarf

10 11 go everywhere
jeans everything but
12 13 wearing scarf

she dont understand but
slowly slowly she understand

she going to school
going home
you know

i dont see her since im here

5 6 years

but i know since that time
shes praying holy quran 5 time a day

same life
we have in the school

cemetery miss you 19

same life

you wake up
you pray study school

mom clean clean
you dont have to do anything

anything

but everything in the house
you want to tell the mom
anything you want to eat and
it will be there

anything

they will be never No
they will be never Wait
they will be never I dont have the money

No

they will be never Whats this 1
its always Ready and

even you dont know
you want to eat this 1
you always have it

you want money
you go mom
go grandmother
go uncle

2 rupees 5 rupees 10 rupee
you get

grandmother
everybody give

cemetery miss you 20

you can get

grandfather die
grandmother alive

she give
you get

my father know she bad 1
before but she change

everybody know
say She change

trust me
i never see a different her
she my grandmother

my whole family live together

uncle cousins
same like me
everybody

so build community
everybody there
man

everybody see you
everybody know

im 2nd biggest 1 so
everybody know

always keep eye on me
because im the big son

the daughter you study
then you go college

not much
just little

so you know

1 year

then you learn home thing

how to cook
how to sew
how to do this kind of thing

at 17 18 19
15 16 not ready
ya
good not go to school very long

only if very rich
or very very poor
she need to study

she can be teacher
or she can get scholarship

otherwise
no fucking way you can be

No No

no will marry woman who works

but she dont have to work after with me
cannot allowed by me to work if she want

my father give me permission

You can marry white woman black woman
Only have to respect us

cemetery miss you 22

Muslim and be with us

my father is a friend
man

talk to him everyday
tell him everything
everything

my mother dont know

my father know
i have the girlfriend in hongkong
my father know i drink alcohol
my father know i smoke
he know i hang around with these jokers and do this shit so

he know
he know i do shit

of course he gonna ask me and
i say No

but he know

my mother great lady
always pray
5 time a day

every day

every year
we have the big pray in the house

everybody come

she make the big pot of rice
we dont celebrate birthday
these kinds of things

but my mother say
You you are the boss of this house

17 18 because i am the big 1

17 18 i start work with my father
in the showroom

of course i dont get the money
just the pocket money

give it to me
pocket money
i hang around with my father

actually

when i start showroom
my father get me the bike
second hand

stay showroom not nice
my job was to go
and collect the moneys from people

payments
that was my job for
15 16 month

my father dont tell me
hang around with zuhayr
the handsome neighbour

father tell me
Dont hang around with him

handsome guy
man
really handsome guy

he use the creams on his face

parents dont want i hang around with him

going on bike
and i get a serious problem
man
a fucking serious problem

i not staying always inside showroom
outside

not listen so much my parents
i have a problem of zuhayr

he fall in love with a lady
my neighbour and
zuhayr have another friend ashraf and

we are 3 together and
i am 17 18
zuhayr 18 19 and
he ashraf is 24

he got his own bike and this kind of stuff

im working but
for my dad
man

we are good friend

im working but
not so much

and he zuhayr fall in love with the girl
and the girl always calling the mobile

but then break up but
that girl still

cemetery miss you 25

calling zuhayr mobile so

make a problem

zuhayr come to me and cry
big problem start from there

but kids thing so

i tell him
Dont do that
my father have a big name in sialkhot
so i can say Hey
Oy

Dont do that

so i say to him Hey
Dont do

ashraf and zuhayr fighting and

then zuhayr pissed off with me because the girls talking now
im disturbing everybody and

now they get me from the house
they get me on the bike and

this guy bilal
bilal dhul is a big guy in pakistan

they do bad things
they do gins

these kinds of things

they shoot people

they bring us and
they drinking alcohol and

they laughing and
they show zuhayr and me guns

they show us but
not pointing guns to shoot us but

laughing and
scaring us and

giving us cigarets and coke and pepsi and
laughing and

after few hours
they tell us Go home but

few days later new things come out
and bilal dhul going to the girls house and

my neighbours and he cannot do anything to me
just cannot touch me

in my neighbours area he cannot touch me

ya
he cannot come and do anything

he cannot do anything

so what have to be
i have to be outside and do something
he cannot be inside my house

and 16 february 430 5 in the morning
in the salat Allahu akbar

16 bullets 2 magazines coming in the house

in the walls
in the washing machine
in the telephones and

cemetery miss you 27

in my bed
through the windows and everything and

nobody knows
nobody notice because

my house in front of the mosque
nobody hear

my mother wake up in the morning and
the prayer and nobody notice

they notice but they just
Hey whats going on

my mother wake up and
she see it
and we dont want to call the police
somebody call the police

somebody shoot in my house
in my house

shoot me
shoot at me
wanting to kill me

Bilal dhul he did it and

my father he cant imagine
he never see this kind of stuff

never police
never

he got gun but
he never shoot it
never try

he got scared

scared security of me

i threaten them
insulting them

saying They can do anything
but They cant do to me

thats the problem
i do this to scare him because

hes taking my friends girlfriend and hes crying and hes putting
cigaret out in hand and
hes drinking alcohol

and getting crazy and
smoking fucking hash and

im getting mad

my mom saying Im in this position in hongkong Because of that
she still saying that word today

You are separate from us because of this guys
This handsome guy zuhayr

very nice guy

i always take care of him
money i always help him

this kind of stuff

the bullet come and

then in the neighbourhood
the story of the girl come out and

then all the men old in the community talking and
then they say i Have to say sorry

my father not
i have to say sorry

my problem
blame come to me

blame come to me

i brought that fight
i make it that fight

my uncles understand
everybody understand

but my father
you know what he do

he go to that mans house and
he put his hands together and

he say to the man Sorry
Give sorry to us

Stay away from our life

i get pissed off from that
fucking pissed off from that

i say Dad
Why you do that

my uncles come from other city
my dads partners come

everybody angry
angry

very angry and

mom say Dont go to showroom 2 days

cemetery miss you 30

Stay home

i say No
get on the bike
go to the showroom
get the gun

go to showroom
got the security

no problem

all day

close the showroom
i come home

everybody ok
everybody go to sleep

i bow my head
whole house not talking anything
whole house very scary and

in the night time
i know im gonna do it

im gonna Do that shit
im gonna Do this shit

Do it
im going to Do it

Need the respect
very very big my father have to bow his head

his son have the this kind of problem and

then my father say 1 thing

my mother sitting
crying
that thing

dad say
dad say Be a bastard
Bow your head and
Dont say anything

Close the matter

Right now
Dont say this rubbish

Then do it
Open the cupboard
Get the gun and do it in front of me

I give you 300 rupees the month
Heres 200 more

For you
For the cigaret

Can you do it in front of me
Can you put the cigaret in your mouth

Do it in front of your mom

and i cant do it

i put my head
i bow down so

father said Go and shoot or shut up
Be the bastard and Be quiet and Go sit down

mom saying Dont do it and
then i have to bow down because

cemetery miss you 32

Respect
man

family respect

dont be the criminal
be the respect and

after you meet this guy
Hi hi
Hi

and then my father get the paper from the court

if anything happen to him
then his fault

bilal dhul responsible and

then after 1 month 15 day i get shot on the bike

two bullet
bullet didnt hit me but in the bike

Boahm Boahm in the bike and

then my father come with partner in the car

get the bike to be repaired
the man trying to scare me
threat me

Stay away from the girl
Stay

but not possible
girl living in front of me

every day see it
every day

cemetery miss you 33

not watching for her but
sometimes cooking and

go to the showroom and
fathers friend give me the gun

buy the bullet
give me the list of names of the money to collect
go to get the money owed

before the collector robbed but
i know how to do it

every day in the morning to the shop and
then the bike 30 35 kilometre to collect the money

always gun with me
of course never take it out

only some people know i have the gun
never take it out and
they treat me like a son

Hey come inside

im a very young guy
im 16 17

they treat me like the small baby
they give me the tea
the food

How your mom your father
Everybody
I dont have the money but
Here take 100 rupees

so every day i make the 600 700 rupees
every day
im the cool guy

cemetery miss you 34

they dont have the money so
they give me 100 200 rupees so

so every day go back to showroom
close
go home

change the clothe
charge the mobile
go out on the bike

leave the mobile at home because
my father always going to call me Where are you

What you doing Come back home so
always leave the mobile at home

not late
10 1030 but

father knows because
hes going to lay there and

hes having to get up and
open the door

so hes angry always

Where the fuck have you been
this kind of stuff

very pissed off

16 february they shoot at me and in april i am in hongkong

in pakistan in 2000
they started the census
make id cards passports
i apply for a passport

i had my id card

my father got idea
for my safety

wanted to send me with a guy to korea

i dont know why
i never wanted to go to that country

What the fuck
i had always wanted to stay in my country and

be like my father
a businessman

my father come home
he tell me i am Going to korea in a few days

my mother and i were laughing
i laughed out loud

he gave me my passport
You are going to go to korea with this guy
From here to hongkong From hongkong to korea

i was shocked
This is not possible

i thought it was a joke
it was when my mom started to cry that i realize it was true

I am going abroad and

i dont want to go
i have not idea what is fucking hongkong
what do people speak

What is english
What is shit

i have no idea and
i have to go
all because
He will take care of me He will take care of me He is resident He
knows everything He will take care of me
and

i dont want to go but
i have to go

i dont want to leave bilal dhul alone like this
i feel pain every day

every day

i cry with my own eyes
just for nothing
just for being too angry with myself

i cant do anything
i just cant do anything
i bite my own hands

i cant do anything

i go and tell my dads friend
also owns a showroom

he smokes a lot of hash and
at that time i dont smoke hash

he wants my dad to spend money on me
2 million 3 million rupees to put a showroom that makes vip
motors too
he wants me to be boss and he a collector

i put it to my dad but
he says he doesnt trust this guy and

You are so young

cemetery miss you 37

I cant do it

were sitting in the main market
at the bus stop

No

This guy tells me to Shoot this guy
Shoot this guy
We can do it

i said No No no
i had everything ready
and this guy tells me to Shoot him

I said No
im going to do it from my own hand

Uncle look
He fuck me over
man

Im going to another country
I really fucking dont want to leave

he said Ok Heres the gun Do it

it was just me
a big shit
only me

i was forcing them to give me a gin
they said they would do it
thats why they are there
i got 2 magazine

i put it in my fucking pants start the bike straight to that mans
house

knock on the door unlock the door

cemetery miss you 38

man come out
auntie come out

his mom
Hi auntie

Is bilal dhul at home

he doesnt know who i am
i enter inside

1 lady is sitting on the floor
shes cooking something

she screams Who are you
Stay outside

a man speaks from inside
Who is that

i take out my gun
his brother is sitting there

i say Not you Dont move

only bilal dhul i shoot at his legs
i shoot 6 bullets in the air and 6 on his feet
on his fucking legs

2 bullets were stuck inside his legs

he is still in a wheelchair
he accepted that he did it

my uncle is the city mayor in faisalabad
it had become mayors problem already
it had become politics problem

my uncle said You mother fucker Is my identity going to be
fucked like this

it became a political problem
my father only cared about 1 thing
security of me

thats why my father want me to leave the country
Be happy

that is it

i take out the gun
i said Whoever are you dont move

i said Boom Boom Boom Boom 12 bullets
i said Fuck you

i dont want to shoot him
im scared

im scared
i dont want to shoot him

Whoever i said
Fuck you
Man

I am here to shoot you Not to listen to you

i shoot him 6 times on the sofa
3 bullets in him

i come out
i put the gun in the back

the gun is heat

i put on my glasses
i take out the key to the bike

start the bike
nicely go from there into the street

cemetery miss you 40

It is respect

i go from there
nobody touches me

i go back to the showroom
tell them Ive done it already

i am happy very happy
that night my dad gave me 500 rupees to go shopping

buy some new shirts for korea

4 oclock i leave my house
i have a flight

i dont know what time 9 or 10 at night
my parents didnt send me

my parents friend send me in a car
my father say If you dont want to go Leave now

No dad
Im going to go
Im going to do it

i have no idea
man
i have no fucking idea

my passport is a fresh 1
theres no stamp anything

no hongkong entry and

i have to go to hongkong
hongkong to korea

when i enter inside
the administration people ask me

How much you pay to abdul nasser
this is my uncle and my dads friend so

im going with him
he ask me to show them how much money i have

i have 1000 us and i show the money and

because he has money
he puts some in my front pocket
his money

in thailand i give him his money

i have only 100 something us and some pakistani rupee
6000 or 7000 rupee like

4 or 500 hongkong dollar

this guy come with me
he fill out all the forms

i dont know how to read and write so
he fill out everything for me

i give him things for his wife from my mom
some nice clothe

in thailand in the middle of the night
early in the morning
we change clothe

he needs to go to hongkong
i need to go to korea

we change planes
hes going to see me there

i know hes running

cemetery miss you 42

i can feel it i can feel it

hes running now

i know that
so okay Fuck you

in thailand i got separate
i came to hongkong airport

everybody
people
follow

pakistani asking me
You dont want to help me
just want to say Go that way

i follow people
i follow the line

i put my face out

im gonna die now

i dont know whats going to be happen

there is a lady
a very beautiful 1

i choose her
follow that line

she ask me Tourist
i look at her

she say Show money

i understand that 1

i show the money
i fucking say Here
man

Here look at that
with my pointer finger

i point to my front pocket Here look

show money show money

she take out 1 fucking stamp
and she goes Tok she said

i go Fuck
What the fuck

Hongkong is coming

i was scared because i dont know anything
every human looks the same thing

all chinese looks like the same thing

the smell
coming from hongkong

i dont like it

i dont like hongkong

im supposed to go korea
i come to hongkong

i dont know how
i know im in hongkong

im in the airport for 7 or 8 hour

this guy was supposed to come

cemetery miss you 44

he didnt come

i know he fucked me

i know hes a hongkong resident
and he has a wife here

he told me where to go but

still

tell me not to write it down
not to say anything
he told me nobody could understand this 1

im standing in the airport
i come out of the airport

i dont know english
i dont even know the difference between Who are you and How
are you

i come out of airport and ask somebody for a cigaret with a point
he give me a cigaret

i smoke it

i dont know where to buy cigaret

i have to be nice to this guy
this smoking guy

i smoke and i think about it

i come out
look at the hongkong mountains

i say What the fuck
This is hongkong with the mountain

cemetery miss you 45

This is fucking hongkong

You call this even hongkong

i look at the buses

What the fuck
Where to go

bus
Where go

i cannot leave

taxi stand
waiting

how people sit in the taxi and
how does the meter work

Fuck

dont have much money
i have rupees

i dont want to change until i see the proper guy who tells me how
much is the value of the
hongkong money

1 taxi guy tells me Oh
You come

hes seen already what i was doing
checking out people

standing there
getting hungry

dont know what to buy
where to buy

cemetery miss you 46

he says Come here
he says Where you from

i dont understand what he said
when he speaks english

i dont know what hes saying but
i know hes saying pakistan

Ya ya
Im pakistan

he points to me how much money
i dont kow how much money

i have rupees and us dollars
he comes in front of me and takes the us dollars

Ok
Us dollars that much
i said Ok

maybe 25 dollars or 30 dollars us
i gave him 2 or 3 us papers

he brings to me sham shui po

i get out
i see 1 pakistani
i feel fucking comfortable

Im in the world back again

i see a pakistani shop
straight go there
buy cigarets capstan

i tell him abdul nasser
he gets me a guy
i tell him about that guy

they know him
hell be here in 1 or 2 day

hes coming from hongkong
so hes here already

he went to korea
and he sent me to hongkong

he had to
he came back to meet me after that because

i had his wifes clothe and
everything

3 or 4 days later

the other guy help me find a place to sleep
so i could live

where im going to live is with these 3 lahore guys
they dont like very much

but i have a passport
i need a passport

everybody tells me to sell the passport

i know the story

you need to sell your passport and ticket
the price for a passport is 3 or 4 grand hongkong dollars

at that time is 25 000 rupees

i know its going to be happen

people trying people looking people doing
in the market

cemetery miss you 48

hes looking for me
hes asking people

so i went to talk to him
What the fuck Why you do like this
i said Look i have to do this 1
he says You need help
You give me 50 hongkong dollars

I dont have money
I had rupees

I gave them to store
They gave me some food and some cigarets

Thats it

I had us dollars
Dollars us and
Theyre also finished from the cigarets and stuff

this is 3 or 4 days only
3 or 4 days

i fucked off with these guys

then that abdul nasser guy brought me 1 day to work
1 day he brought me to work
give me the money

where i live for 6 days
i give it to them

to start to pay to them and be a good guy
but i dont like them

they treat me like a shit

i come to hongkong
i dont know anything

they fucking push their feet at me when im sleeping

Smell of hongkong
its disgusting
the stink
i want to vomit

i dont want to eat anything

they tell me not to stay in hongkong

1st time somebody sends me to buy something from 7 11
You gonna take and then pay or
Pay first and then take

i have no fucking idea
they give me 10 dollars and

they give me a ball and tell me to go and buy yogurt from the
street

1 more guy come new in hongkong
lot of visa scam because visa is free so

a lot of people come
a lot of pakistani tourist come

im dealing only with pakistan people
they look chinese but
not chinese

everybody looks the same
i leave that house

i think about leaving hongkong

its quite strange

not much money
hungry

cemetery miss you 50

cry

only 1 time

when i meet that guy he helps me to call at home
i call home

i cry
the 1st time i listen to my mom i start to cry

i got hungry for 1st time in my life

the whole day i do not eat
i lie down at night time in the bedroom
crying because i dont have the food

i live with somebody but
i dont want to say I dont have money

im so tired
from walking and walking everywhere

they dont give me the house key
i walk everywhere to find a job in the street

i have a place in sham shui po

im looking for a job and waiting for the trucks

and then that guy
abdul nasser who
brought me to hongkong

i have a 14 day visa
he help me to stamp my passport already

ive been in hongkong 11 or 12 day already
by that time

in 12 days

cemetery miss you 51

i change my room already

live with some different people
cool people from lahore and
some nice people from my city sialkot

they helped me to live and eat

they tried to tell me where to get a job
to help me

this kind of stuff
this guy help me

i dont have a passport
i had to sell it

I need some money

this guy helped me to sell the passport for dollar 3350 hongkong
he gave me 50 dollar

3300 dollar he said that he was going to send to his house

he didnt send it

he keep it

i talk to my dad
he talk to my dad

I bring your son into hongkong I need something so
he keeps that and
then hes suddenly gone again

hes a resident
hes got a wife here

he brought me to his house also

cemetery miss you 52

i saw his very old wife

they give me some gow gee
fried vegetable saag
fried saag and wild rice

fuck

i dont want to eat that
im not eating in hongkong

i smell the disgusting smell of hongkong
the street

people
chinese

chinese have smell

i cannot eat

in pakistan
they have also but

they have something different

its a weird smell
everywhere it smells in hongkong

folder b file 5: 52 min 18 sec

i was living in sham shui po

no visa
no passport
no money
no anything

this guy sells my passport to 1 of the guys who win 96 000
hongkong
he buy my passport for 3350 dollar to go back to pakistan
because his face
look same to me

he get the passport and says I will send the money to your father

i say Alright
he will send it

i dont know how to do it

he didnt send the money to my parent

my father asked him and
he said At least i bring your son abroad
It costs little bit to me

now im stuck there with no visa

first thing
Dont get close to the police

Dont see the police

get scared
get away

need to stand in 1 sham shui po area
need to wait for the big truck and container

they will pick you up and you can go do loading and unloading

i dont understand language
i have no idea what the fuck is empty or

the ticket to everything
the 7 11 or some shit

cemetery miss you 54

Tiu ne mo lo

i eat but not much
i dont like the smell

i dont like the food
the cooking

even to cook at home but
its not nice food
i have to go to restaurant but
its still expensive

like banana
coke
this kind of stuff

snack food

difficult
fucking difficult

the first place they bring me to see
tsim sha tsui star ferry

stuck in the tsim sha tsui star ferry

only understand in hongkong tsim sha tsui star ferry and sham
shui po

tsim sha tsui star ferry What the fuck i see

im a muslim

im new guy come to hongkong
sold his passport have no fucking id

fucking indonesians
girls

for me that time
a girl is dancing in star ferry for me

What the fuck is going on here
man

ya great

but after 2 hour 3 hour
i must to sit down

Where the fuck i am
What the fuck is going on

Where i am

i wanted to get the bus to go back home and
i dont know how to go back

thats how i begin to learn in hongkong

everybody have a girlfriends
every body works this way

hard work

sometimes you get the job
asking everybody and

every motherfucking pakistani dont want to be help you

nobody want to help you

at that time a lot of tourist go because hongkong had entry

everybody look the same
even if you get arrest you could use somebody passport to come
out

they look similar
the faces

like for the first time you come to hongkong
you looks

every chinese looks the same

pakistanis look the same way
man

so people come out and everybody has visa and
this kind of stuff

sham shui po was
difficult

1st was nice because new guy
i want to learn

now im fucking alone there
nobody want to help me

they call that place karay
to stand

i stand like 22 day

straight
man

1 month i stand there and
i only get 1 time go to the job from there and
1 or 2 time somebody bring me

so what youve got
200 300 dollar all day working and

that 200 300 youre going to have to give him the next 2 or 3 days
thats all the money you make

cemetery miss you 57

you get so
so fucked and total fucked up

have no idea

crying
1st time
in hongkong
for food

i dont know
its like most bad time and

where im living this guy tell me
If you dont get the money

because 1 month i pay rent but
1 month i didnt have the money to pay rent so

he give me 1 month notice and told me If you dont pay the price
You got to move out

another guy from my city
he said No

Hes not going to go
Hes going to stay with us

but still
its like 1 1/2 month already i didnt pay the rent so
theyre pissed off at me
even my friend was pissed off at me

i dont have work
i want to work
they know that so

i feel like shit
man

cemetery miss you 58

they have to pay the rent
they need to have a guy in the house who can share with them
and pay the rent so

he didnt kick me out
he kept my luggage and i left that place
that time i dont know tauqeer and
know everybody

i hear already but
i dont know everything

i go to the star ferry

still i cannot speak english
of course i can say Hi Hello How much

Tiu ne lo mo
Tiu ne lo mo

Fuck you in chinese

this kind of word i only know in 3 month
2 month
2 month

no house no money nothing
dont have anything
10 dollar dont have
nothing have

got few pant
few shirt

1 jacket only
in guy house

got nothing

got a lot of pakistani Hello Hello Hello but

cemetery miss you 59

you got nothing motherfuck
if you dont have money

1st to have money is to get a little bit from somebody
250 dollar and
then 1 day work also but

i live more than 20 day in star ferry
i sleep there

tsim sha tsui star ferry
i sleep there

1st 3 4 day is just like
Ya

but after that

my heart cry every night

Where the fuck i am

then i call back home

say Im fine I have a house Am living there with some friend
Everything
Sleep in there

even then theyre saying If youre not comfortable there
Not happy there
Come back

my father say this 1

Like
Ok

otherwise
you go there

cemetery miss you 60

do hard work

do everything but
the other side is saying this 1
Youre not happy
You can come back
You got a problem then come

No problem

You cant have everything but

No
Come

1 time were gonna do something
cry man

until 12 oclock 1 oclock you have to sleep and
then you have to look at the stars

slowly
slowly

money finished also
man

no money and
have to sleep there and

have to wait for other people
man

i pray to god that they leave the rice box and i can pick up and i
can eat that 1

they leave their mcdonald and

i pick it up
i eat that 1

cemetery miss you 61

i drink the water from the public toilet in tsim sha tsui

i live there
i sleep there more than 20 day

nobody have this kind of time i hope but

i see very bad time in star ferry
tsim sha tsui

theres me

more people sleep
man

more
chinese poor people

more people newspaper
sleep also

people with cardboard
they lie down on the floor then
they cover their head with the cardboard and
they sleep there

no blanket
nothing

anything

its illegal to sleep in there

6 oclock 7 oclock theyre gonna start the duty and
everybody move

everybody move before
everybody move already
so

cemetery miss you 62

cry

no food
hungry

sleepy

clothe dirty

how you take shower
how you change your clothe

sunday
the girlfriend stay

everybody free
i can go to their house

they can cook the nice food
i can eat

because my luggage is there
i can change my clothe

i can take shower
i can do whatever i want

girlfriend
their friends

come over
everything

sleep live 20 day like this and
then get a job from somebody

1 2 day together
like 1200 dollar i get

get that 1200 dollar
straight go back to the same house in sham shui po and
say I want to live with you guys
pay the money

Alright

i give them the 1200 dollar

slowly slowly i would get another job
1 2 day only

not much

fucking in 1 month
2 day

just like this
thats it

that much only
still again nothing
just to eat or
pay the fucking rent

just like this
they will give you the job
that much only

still again nothing

i live with them 15 day 1 month like this
nothing again

and then
no food no money

again

fucking same thing

cemetery miss you 64

same situation again
this time its the same thing i do it

3 month hongkong already
didnt do anything

back to the sham shui po garden

1 day very very fast raining
im wearing slipper

im wearing
not nice clothe im wearing

its like 1130 12 oclock in the night
sham shui po garden the top

like a bridge
cover
with the rain
everything is cover

im sleeping there

i hear 2 pakistani guy coming
i hate hash drugs like

in our family nobody use drug
i always stay away from drug people

alcohol
i dont drink alcohol in pakistan

i smoke cigaret
i just chill

eat nice food
chill guy

i listen to music but

not this kind of fucking drug

i stay away from these kind of people

i can see some pakistani guys coming
1 is good looking

wearing nice clothe
wearing a necklace and

drunk and screaming and jumping

they come closer under there because its raining
they come

they sit there

they start to roll a joint
they didnt bother me

few minute
hour

after that they feel it
that im pakistani in there

Hey Who are you Come here Who are you What are you doing
in here

i say Look
man

Like this
Like this
Like this

they ask me What city you from
i said Im from sialkot

cemetery miss you 66

they say Youre fucking me Youre from my city and Youre
sleeping under here
Sleeping in here in the garden

Whats your name
Where you live
Tell your father name

they said Isnt father named tawfeek sahib
i said Ya

they said my father is abdul rabahji
i said They told me somebody is here but
I have no idea who the fuck are you

in this kind of way go on

its not really a relative because
its far fucking relative
my father know his father through his grandfather
something this way

in this way we know each other

our families dont know each other
we dont go to each other house

were not close family
i know him that way

he said Ok
Go to my house and sleep in here

i ate with him
whole day i hang around with him

until the night
went to his house to sleep

morning time

cemetery miss you 67

wake up
take shower

he saw i didnt have clothe
he tells his friend to give me clothe
i wear the clothe

he says Lets go out

i go out with him
where he go
eat in a restaurant

1 day no problem
keep quiet
2 days

same thing again and
then they tell me

Look you understand what im doing
i say Ya youre selling hash
Man

he says Ya these are the bullets
You buy for this much

i say I know the market already
Where you do it i understand already

he said You give each bullet
You make 20 dollar
Im gonna make 30 40 dollar

they get the hash from china
the hash come from pakistan
by road

who deliver here
how deliver here

cemetery miss you 68

i have no idea

i have no idea

people call him
in his mobile
on his name tauqeer bhai

i am saajidji
the delivery guy

wherever you want
i have to deliver it in hongkong

where i do deliver
sometime people give 10 dollar for the transportation
other time they dont give but
from him
i got a house
for living free

with the friend
with the guys

i got a restaurant
to eat
every day

sometime maybe i can get the card
get the cigaret pack

fake 1
not nice 1

fake thing
this way

he tell me he gonna give me some money end of the month
like 1000 dollars 1500 dollars
10 000 rupee to send it in pakistan

cemetery miss you 69

this 1
he did it like

maybe
fucking
1 time 2 time

he make so much money
never give me cash but
give me everything

eat drink wherever you want

this kind of thing
this kind of stuff you have always
but you dont get fucking cash much
100 dollars 200 dollars cash here or

100 200 hundred cash
300 here

but
not much

so hang around start with tauqeer
man

understand the fucking business life
how hes work
he get the credit

people come from china
china to come in here

i make bullets
understand the business already with him
in 1 month with him

1 month 2 month
living and everything with him

cemetery miss you 70

fucking star ferry

lot of indonesian
having the sex with them

learning the hongkong life

wearing the dodgy clothe
g

big things
with the big pant
with the dragon
this kind of stuff
wearing

he buy
he pay money

what you want to buy
go to mongkok buy

so

very nice but

no cash

but respect
got respect

everybody
everywhere you go
Tauqeer brother
everywhere you go

Saajid
Tauqeer brother

no problem

cemetery miss you 71

in here have a
kowloon side
used to have a pakistani gangster

when i was not fucking arriving here
i just heard their names

1 of them is savvy and
1 of them is luqmaan bah

tauqeer used to work for savvy and
after he worked for luqmaan bah
the last few years but

not anymore

that time
tauqeer was a big name
a big hash

talk about a big name
sayf udeen
a big hash and

jordan got another guy
his name is izz basaam

we call them jordan guys

they got cars rented
got good money
the job cars everything
these good guys

there are 2 gangs only and
we are all together

in kowloon side

in hongkong

cemetery miss you 72

lan kwai fong
wanchai

whats going on
that shit
that we dont know

in kowloon side
everything is us

you need to buy drugs
in kowloon
you buy from us

we got the market

you got to listen to the story
its very interesting man

tauqeer give me 2 1/2 3 kg to roll in a month
to roll to make a bullet
to do it

living with the guys
little money problem
little this problem

i got this problem

got a girlfriend
i got it a little bit good life
right

where i dont have to worry about eating
living
this kind of shit

not got any saving or some money but

if youre a drug dealer

cemetery miss you 73

all is good

i was not smoking even
not even smoking

always hanging around the middle of the night
go with him out
saturday night go to disco
he pay the money
free everything

gods enjoying overstay motherfucker
in hongkong enjoying the gods

doing everything

but how you like doing like this
like you know
live like how boss live

he have a girlfriend always with him
live with him

im tauqueer
his 2 fucking mobiles

we dont see sun
we sleep at that time

we wake up night time
6 oclock in the evening
6 oclock i have to give the duty

2 oclock in the night
we gonna have a lunch break

have to call in to the hotel
have to collect 22 chapatis
with 5 3 6 kind of different curries

pick up the food
how many guys eating

go to disco
everybody drink
everybody smoke
we give them money
a lot of stuff
2 2.5 kg

i fucking deliver
only in 1 month

it goes good
slowly slowly everything fine

i take care of it already
i take care the business already

he dont have to do much
run much

he just little deals with china
i can handle it
all the dealer

hes sleeping

everything i know
then life
everything going fine

we got little more bigger
we got more
more people

when you want where you want how much you want
i can handle all that

fighting

cemetery miss you 75

lots of people get your stuff and dont give you the money

get a fight
go there
come back
this kind of stuff going on

that life is going fine with a little bit more because we have more
people coming and
sitting together

big gang already
many people
a lot of people

sham shui po garden
they are eating there

night time only

everybody finish their work
they come here to buy from their boss

he gave them money and
they pay me to buy drugs

i give to my boss and
i make money

we find 1 more guy
he also from my city
he also know tauqeer

he starting a business
now he trying to take my place
which i dont want

he got it
little
much closer for

cemetery miss you 76

3 or 4 days

i dont do anything
i live in his house but
i dont go with him

he feel that

Saajid i get you a room

he says Fuck that Here i got you a room Your own room We
living in here We need to
get the house without drug

the 3 or 4 kg thats in the house is very bad
its not good

we get a house just to put the stuff
1 key tauqeer have
1 key i have

my tv is there and
only the mattress on the floor

for bullet packing only
some music in this 1 only
nothing

pillows
no

nothing

just the house

only where you get it
put your stuff

play my music
alone

nobody can go with me there
nobody

hongkong is in here
and im rolling the fucking bullets

thats my job
keep going

quiet
slowly slowly music

thats how they fucking do it

pick up
go there
go

how many other
do that 1

give the stuff
give back
give back
that much
that much
go back

bring it back
this kind of things im doing

and
ahh

that put me separate
a little bit

and then tauqeer got rich
man
hes a rich guy now

cemetery miss you 78

hes got a car

i
man

going in cars
coming in cars with
the guys

going here
going there

buying nice clothes

can afford 7 800 dollar pant
7 800 dollar a shirt

he can afford it now
this kind of stuff going on

buying shoe for 800 hongkong
2200 hongkong dollar buying the shoe

can afford that much fucking money
no problem

at the time
nobody
not even think about it

no 1 think about it
just go that way

like this

sell for him 1 kg of hash in wanchai for 20 000 hongkong dollar
we buy it for 8000 hongkong dollar

you see
you want to make somebody happy

cemetery miss you 79

so you give him 9000 hongkong dollar
all the money so

the profit 11 000 hongkong dollar so

and then he give me 5000 hongkong dollar and
then hes happy

he gave me 5500
500 extra
my profit give me

we were sitting in the big apple
in wanchai
he tells me Buy a drink for everybody

theres 26 27 people

after we got 2 car
and 1 bike

he tells Make the full tanks and
Pay the money from there so

he use my money

he want to drink at the top of the peak

like you know
6 guys 7 guys here

got the hash

1/2 kg in here
You are my guys

i do nothing
like tauqeer

tauqeer do nothing

im tauqeer guy

just hang around with tauqeer
tauqeers right hand just

always with him

Tonight 9 oclock
I want to drink from the top on the peak

Lets go

Now

I want go to stanley

we were sitting in the big apple
right now

enjoying drinks paying money doing stuff
hiding

fucking things going on in the street
there are always fights

i always there but
i have no fucking idea whats going on but
im always there

we fight also
a lot of fighting in hongkong
but never got myself

i never fight
for myself

tauqeers the kind of guy whos like
I wanna go now to stanley

have that much money

cemetery miss you 81

that much position already

the new guy whos inside
from my city
his name is mahdy

mahdy got problem

tauqeer wearing a necklace and this kind of stuff

however
that mahdy and tauqeer arrested

tauqeer come to the prison 18 month

that i know

to collect

tauqeer 18 month prison
blame it on tauqeer because of some illegal stuff on tauqeers
name

thats why

its the illegal passport
yes

its illegal passport
coming to his name and

thats 18 month prison
and that new guy

mahdy said Ok i will accept Thats my passport
every month tauqeer come up

that new guy mahdy had 18 month prison

tauqeer say he Cant forget that

cemetery miss you 82

he Cannot forget what he did for him

he
mahdy
in the prison

tauqeer he sent for him the things
he give mahdy more things
he take care of him

even without him asking
he sent some money to his family

to his home
also without asking him

after that tauqeer arrested finally
with the drugs

i was sorry then

he got to leave prison
and he had to go back

back to pakistan

2 guys living with us
their marriages is coming so
they must have go back

im 1 year in hongkong
december coming already

november november
tauqeer arrested

i have 1/2 kg

the house where were living
those guys all want to move

only 1 wants to stay here and
1 moving for work

all the 4 guys are going to pakistan because
they have already girls
they stay there for 5 6 years

theyre all neighbours from 1 street
theyre all going back

so i got no house again
i have that room that tauqeer paid
but i need to pay the rent and everything

luckily
i got 1/2 kg
less than 1/2
i have it

tauqeer wants to buy a customer clothe

everything shit on
lifes fucked up

i start to sit

1st
i live in sham shui po
trying to make that room good

for living there like 1 month
i dont know who is the landlord

the landlord come
pay the money 1 time so
that i can live 1 more month

i live that month

cemetery miss you 84

after that i take the house
i move to chungking for 3 4 months

no
not even 2 month

i pay 1 month
after that i dont know
man

i just live for few days

i sit in star ferry

again

not much money
not allowed to buy anything

i have 1/2 kg but
not much customer

the people who know me
i give a little bit
and then get the money |

tauqeer in pakistan already

after 28 days call tauqeer
he in pakistan 28 days already

tell him

he said Ok use the money If you have money send me
If no

I know
Ok
Understand

cemetery miss you 85

i say Everything is fucked up
Everything fucked up

he said he Need to rest now little bit

that means the whole plan is fucked

i have the 1/2 kg

i start to sit in star ferry
start to sit in star ferry

that time i can understand a little bit of english already

Hello Hi How are you

we can talk about indonesian girlfriends
filipina girlfriends
we can speak a little bit in english

not much but
you can communicate with somebody that way

star ferry i was living

and the very nice guys from karachi i meet them
i meet the guys

somebody bring them in hongkong
they have they bring a guy in here with them
they are from karachi
they study

they come by a junk

he bring them here for 150 000 hongkong
they come to china and from china they by junk in here

they have china visa so

cemetery miss you 86

in china they meet 1 more guy
that guys from quetta
that guy is afghani guy

haytham
haytham has his own company of hash

you know
theyre growing there

own factory
that kind of stuff

they have to make a hash with a machine and
everything
hes a businessman

he comes to do business in china
they brought him

his factory is in pakistan

they bring him into hongkong and

these guys meet me and

i know the agent
i have to get a room for them
i get the house for them
they are living there

i explain them everything and
i live with them
chungking is not a very nice place for me

they like to smoke hash also
i give them to smoke

the beginning of my smoking

i actually forgot

when i was with tauqeer somebody bet me

on my birthday

15 june

he said Ok

i make cigaret for tauqeer on my hand and give it to him

he always play card
haytham always ask me because i dont play cards
he says What are you doing saajid

Nothing boss

Ok got nothing to do
Make a cigaret

even though i dont smoke
im going to make a cigaret for him

the guy tells me Youre making
When you gonna smoke

i say Never

he bet with me that in 1 year i will do it
Today is 15 june Your birthday next 15 june You will do it

i said Ok
Man
Lets see

and thats true

i didnt smoke like i did it but
i smoke like

cemetery miss you 88

Puff it

i was moving and
that guy was communicating good things with me
good fucking things happen with that guy

he brought
that haytham guy
he had a lot of fucking money

he had to go back to china
he goes back to china

i call tauqeer
i keep them calm and

tauqeer is like Coming coming coming
i have to make them Wait wait wait

theyre dealers

the 2 guys just come to hongkong to work
that guy is dealer
haytham the dealer

these are my parties
i make the deal
tauqeer is not here

im holding them
give the lemon tea the food
My boss is coming His flight is coming Wait wait wait

haytham need to go to china
man
He need to do his shit so

he go to airport
he go to pakistan and
he have to come back to china again

cemetery miss you 89

thats haytham

the next day he leave
he live our house only 2 days

tauqueer leaving
haytham leaving
and another guy leaving

haytham goes to pakistan
hes a rich guy

he has us dollar and everything
a rich guy

karachi guys in here
theres a good steady guys
trying to teach me also

they always study computer and
they want to learn chinese

they cannot find work

theys a piece of shit
they cant do anything

i play with them computer games in the cafe

this kind of stuffs

im holding them
theyre nothing but
theyre attached with haytham

tauqeer
however
come to china

i tell him to Meet haytham

cemetery miss you 90

he says No time
I have to come to hongkong

he comes to hongkong
but haytham is there already

i forgot his names
Whats this other guys names

but haytham is there already
now he brings them here

i let them meet haytham
they are ishaq and attiq
they from the karachi guys

he meet them
they didnt know about anything

about hash or anything but
Haytham will hook you up
Hes a nice guy

Dont give us anything but
Give us something to eat
500 dollar 1000 dollar

that sort of thing

make a deal no problem
hes my friend

whatever you want to do
do it

they have visa also
everybody has visa

tauqueer come back
go to china

cemetery miss you 91

come back

they also go to china come back go to china come back go to
china come back just need
the money and
apply the visa in wanchai

you have free visa so
they have visas and
the guy looks like me

1 guy
his name is noman
he from also karachi

i have his papers
i have his passport

he looks like me little bit

i use his passport
you can imagine

i go to fucking china
bring it 1/2 kg of hash with me in my fucking bag
on somebody passport

and then

because this guys
all people have to show

we are businessmen
we are making entry in hongkong so

they believe you more
they give you 14 day visa

if they believe you little bit they dont accept you

cemetery miss you 92

you learn to play
have to show money
what business youre doing

in english encounter

dont make satisfied
they give you 6 day 7 day visa
that means they dont be satisfied with you
7 day visa they give you

that means in 6 days
you have to go back again to entry
spend the money and

even to work in hongkong
you dont have the money to entry back and
you fuck up your visa just because of that 1 and

you want to leave and
you have to sell your passport because of that 1

i got arrested
that guy send me passport
i got very brave

i get not scared anymore not scared anymore like no more scared
inside

this guy get the passport and i go to fucking china
on somebody passport

he dont have money
i get his passport go to china get 14 day entry come back

actually
tauqeer friend come back

i let them meet tauqeer

cemetery miss you 93

go back again
he makes a deal in there

he bring 1 kg
he has to go every 14 days
man
because visa is for 14 days
every 12 13 days he has to go
even he wants or dont want

everybody has visa
man

like every second person has visa

some of them dont have it
some dont have visa
overstay also

tauqeer brings 1/2 kg

people borrow passports
people checked by cops a lot

we have a guy
we call Shah shah
Uncle uncle dobaaraa

his name is this because every day
he comes and get check again
man

we have 1 more also
uncle gaith

in hongkong these are our people

overstays
illegals

cemetery miss you 94

uncle gaith
hes gone

wherever he goes
hes lost man

so hes going to call you Hey man im lost again

Where are you

Man
Im right here its the fucking white building right next to 1 more
big building and next to that 1 more building and right there

theres a very nice guy also
hes fucking inspector
hes coming and living with me

life is going on
he comes to hongkong

hes a police inspector

he fucked up his job
he resigned it
come to hongkong

hes a big guy with mustache with pakistani suit

hes coming in the house so
we respect him and call him Uncle

he says Dont call me uncle Call me parsa sahib so
we call him Parsa sahib

parsa sahib share everything
he had 14 day visa

for 14 days he share everything

cemetery miss you 95

he have to buy 1 pant and shirt because
he was wearing pakistani clothe

he shave because he saw the girls coming in the house and
everybody shagging so
he got interested
Ok im going to be also like 1 of these guys
Got a girlfriend or something

shave
get ready
wear a shirt

looks very dirty
very different

ha

cool guy man

after 14 days
his visa finishes

he dont want to sell

he wants to stay here
make some money

14 days

hes arrested

today is 14 day
he goes out 12 oclock and hes arrested already and

he calls me

im sitting with tauqeer
1230 1 oclock
we take the car straight to the sham shui po police station

cemetery miss you 96

a walking pakistani guy comes along from the house wearing the
short and
gives to tauqeer 2 passport
1 passport tauqeer puts in his pocket
1 passport he bring it inside

2 guys come out

tauqeer comes out

Thats brilliant tauqeer
I dont know how the fucking you do inside
You are the man

he said Saajid you are the man
You did it

i said Man
I done nothing

that pakistan guy
no alcohol
no smoke

nothing

very gentle guy
praying in the morning

wake up
pray also

hes almost 1 1/2 2 months in hongkong already
he got no girlfriend
no fucking things

he tries to find work
1 or 2 day he work only

he want to fucking go back

cemetery miss you 97

I will surrender
he has no food even
cant get anything

I have everything there
House
Wife
Everything

Its not nice in here

that guy eat a lady finger
the vegetable
the long 1
the beans

when he eat its stuck in his penis
he cannot piss

No you dont have a passport and
its 2 oclock in the night

even you want to help him

we are sitting in stanley beach
230 3 oclock in the night
and he calls

he dont want a drink
he dont want to do anything
he dont want to drink even water but

hes very full

tauqeer said Drink beer please
he says Can not Can not I will die but Can not

tauqeer says Just try
Just drink beer man Just drink beer It will come out Trust me

cemetery miss you 98

Just hold your nose like a medicine
Just put it inside

he drink 2 glass of beer
he got to barf and

he got pissed
man

he got pissed

anyways

he surrender
he go

he surrender at sham shui po police station
hes surrender

he go back to pakistan

im telling about the 1 guys story only

i like him
i have a 1000 of peoples

i know them
theyre nice guys and

theyre gone

ive been hongkong for 7 year 2 month already
in pak kok

im going to be 8 years in hongkong already

meet 1000 of people

i believe i meet every kind of person and every country
plus pakistani every kind of city

cemetery miss you 99

learning from them 1 by 1

when i was living star ferry
im cry
dont get no sleep
at that time

im not drinking
maybe drink beer but

full beer would be fucking impossible for me to drink
dont smoke hash
lots of crying

looking at the life sitting in star ferry in the dock in tsim sha tsui
looking at the hongkong light and crying

they all have it
these fucking haram people and
i dont have it

1 day you will be me
i clean my tears

1 day i will have
i know i will have

and i wait

you dont have a fucking slipper and you dont have a house

youre hungry
you miss your parent

you have nothing
and youre crying

sometime loading and unloading

sometime

cemetery miss you 100

loading somebody house

construction not much because for construction you need proper
id

when i got in the drugs business
i dont need have tauqeer there

tauqeer 1 time go back

come back business start again

business lost again

18 kg come

i become fucking 50% partner because i handle the stuff
18 kg come from china and tauqeer still have visa

in only few month tauqeer fucked up again

he arrested
its fight

somebody chucked tauqeer in here
cut it in here and cut it in here because

tauqeer abuses savvy
savvy who before was a fucking gangster in hongkong

he have hongkong chinese wife and
he have a china chinese wife

he said he living there

hes from sialkot
he born in my neighbourhood

now he live in lahore
he has a wife in pakistan

in sialkot
my city

he live in lahore
he is saajid name also

his body
full of tattoos

he also wear glasses
short guy
short hair

i believe here in hongkong sitting 1 guy name luqmaan bah
a pakistani guy

everybody think hes the most bastard guy ever come to do his
work

i believe savvy

who using

hes the fucking mastermind

many dont use drug

like use drugs
smoke hash
ya

drink beer
ok
but hes arrested when tauqeer was there in china and
theyre coming and going and everything

hes arrested
96 000 yuen give in the police station in china and bring him out
in shenzhen police
station

cemetery miss you 102

how big power he is like
how much money you can get it 1 time like
96 000

this was in 2002 2003 2002
that time

a lot of money that time
96 000 yuen

that time that was me
imagine that kind of stuff

tauqeer got accident in china
in the fucking bike
broke his bones

he had to live in china
spend lot of money

all the hash fucking money go there
plus lots in there

he make gold chains
everything

we buy a car
we get fucking overstays

im a fucking partner now
18 kg of hash
front of me

im the boss
tauqeer says Everybody talk
You dont give the money
You dont do this 1
You gotta do this 1 now
Have a punishment for you

what can i do

I dont need to go to you
You need to come to me
When you come here You do the punishment

like
You gotta buy drink for everybody now
Ok do this 1 now

this kind of stuff but

if something happen to me
its like What about saajidji

Saajid have sorry for everything
Everything for saajid is ok

Whatever he want to do
Whatever he want to do

i pick up 100 gram
i just give it to somebody

i give it to indonesian girl
she want to sell
i just give it to her

guy got fucked What the fuck man

i said Go and
Talk to tauqeer
Ask him

I dont know how much you buy
8 kg stuff

he said That price

i say How much you looking for

he said That much
he said If you dont talk how much you want to smoke

he had that much money

Can i give you
You dont talk
i said Ok

he asked me for 30 000 thousand
i give him 42 000 dollar
cash

not 1 time

heres 5000
heres 3000 dollar
heres 5000
heres 3000

like this
last i leave

everybody eat
everybody happy
every day beer
every day hash
every day girl
every day enjoyment
every day disco

everything fuck off

every day
people eat food
tauqeer meet peoples there

tauqeer fucked again
in the visa

he have to go to pakistan
tauqeer fucked and

im alone again

fucked
nothing

actually what happened that that fucking guys
karachi guys
they were trying to fuck up tauqeer with other guys

they have fight start in china
theres a fight in china

these guys have a friend hin in china in there so
this kind of communication and this kind of stuff start so

these guys also gone already

i still got the house in the sham shui po
cheung sha wan with
labeeb and together

this karachi guy is gone already

tauqeer also arrested

we buy 13 000 dollar car
10 000 tauqeer give
thats 3000 i give

13 000 dollar car we buy from ishaaq
ishaaq works in the fucking container

load container in the ship
he got his own car
honda car

he sell it to tauqeer as a friendship

very cheap 1
13 000

every night
ishaaq

tauqeer cant drive so
ishaaq have to drive

ishaaq tauqeer and me
me in backseat

always tauqeer have a girl so have to sit in front
very small 1
her name is leena

shes from indonesia but
she speaks our language

she wears this
like
not burka
big scarf and

jeans

shes very
like

hip hop
you know

hip hop girl

tauqeer is fucking tall like this and she is very
like
fucking in here and

she is always there

guy go Saajid i believe tauqeer tell you to fucking turn the car
upside down You can do it
You can do it

and i always have a knife
man

and i always have a knife
have to carry it with tauqeer

everything can happen

tauqeer comes from china
he buys 3 chetes

big fucking machetes

a fucking sword like this

3 for 1000 yuen with papers and everything

bring it in hongkong because of a fight problem there
so bring it

fight happens

they check tauqeer
with the fucking knife

they dont want to do with tauqeer
they come and ask somebody else

its ramadan
they just opened the ramadan then

they come there
after the fasting

like 630 7 oclock they come and say Hey you come out

cemetery miss you 108

because he was using in the market
the day before that to savvy Hey who is savvy in here

everybody drunk
we dont have a problem

that guy come and sit with us
eating food in the restaurant

these guys come in the taxi
savvy have his own taxi

he can get the guys anywhere he wants
things are still very strong

right now very fucking serious strong because hes not staying
out here

now he have other guy to stay in here and
thats luqmaan bah brother fadl ullah

people call him fadah

his english name is savvy
we call him savvy
all the people are pakistani
half chinese but

when chinese come its always with tauqeer
have some filipino
its always Lets go and meet jordan gang
who are once again coming from hongkong to meet in sham shui
po and carry some stuff

3 girls are coming to sham shui po garden

pakistani is also inside
chinese is also inside
english gweilos

all inside but
you dont talk to them youre just getting a deal you dont get close
you dont talk about any
shit

we have our own community
you have your own community

no business deals
no fucking things

teach me 1 by 1
teach me you fucker
you fucker

you fucking saajid
were going to use you and

everybody use and
im very fucking nice

i help everybody

no problem
brother
first i help you

my father was not asking me for the money so what i make i eat

hes working here
everything tastes good
im a happy man

im still not happy
man
im still not happy

god give me very very good time in hongkong
thats why i make 30 000 hongkong dollar just to sleep at home

cemetery miss you 110

i can make that much
i used to be able to make that 1

i did it 1 month but its usually
like
6 or 7

1 month
just hit it and i had like 30 000 dollar just to sleep at home

now im not bad but
i make 600 dollar every night just to sleep at home

every night

money come
very nice
every day

that money go
every day

very fast
very easy

from folder b file 6: 3 min 35 sec

you are happy
man

you have your house
man

a fucking visa

not like fucking animal running in the street

drinking beers in the fucking street

cemetery miss you 111

i pray god ask him give 3000 dollar the month when i was in
sham shui po
i have 3000 dollar i ask give me 5000

i come back from pakistan i have 5000 dollar i pray god give me
6 7000 salary

i have apartment with cece on lamma
i make 7000 8000 dollar

everything easy

food everything
sex everything

im 10 000 salary im not happy

im not happy
man

thank god now i make 12 000 dollar salary
2008
man

2008 november i make 28 000 but
im still not happy

now im not happy in that way
i have other way

everything i want
i want to eat what i want
i want to have a fucking sex with 5 6 womans

i can have what i want
who i want to say a fucking guy to fuck i can say

whatever i want do i can do
whoever i want to do nice and good i can do that 1

cemetery miss you 112

who i want to make happy i can do but
whatever i do im still not happy

its sunday you have your holiday everything you want to do you
do that 1 your girlfriend
coming over you cleaning doing that 1 still

not happy

that time long time very different
that time learning everybody teach me slowly step by step that
time different now i know
everything

now i dont learn that

my brother ataa time

hongkong fuck me
man
make me not normal people man
not normal
you say its animal

that guy was a nice guy praying at home eating a moms food
everything nice even you do
you do bad you think about it before
dont abuse anybody

i come to hongkong come to lamma and you know everybody
call by name everybody
call by these things Hi jacob Hi thomas Hey simon and
everybody know saajidji
everybody know who the fuck is saajidji

but nobody know saajidji

from folder b file 8: 4 min 14 sec

i want to be a good man but
i dont have the time

from folder b file 9: 12 min 14 sec

back in hongkong i piece of shit

Who make me this 1

You

from folder b file 10: 1 min 32 sec

Nobody gets my recording

from folder b file 13: 3 min 8 sec

nothing to everything in 1 day
boss

folder b file 14: 0 min 20 sec

from folder b file 15: 5 min 30 sec

good life
money
bullets

dont have anything

cemetery miss you 114

fragments from folder b file 16: 17 min 34 sec

no feeling
black heart
bad guy

haram halal mix
brother
cannot keep it

Its working
Man

Tell me when its working

fragments from folder b file 17: 17 min 9 sec

why tell me when its me

ive done fucking a lot
everything already

things to do
sisters married
father to mecca

family first

now i dont want to go

i will make aziz name
respect name

make you stand

saajidji will take care of you
gone
miss you

you stand them up

from folder b file 28: 1 min 36 sec

i dont know how to talk with the recorder on

i dont

i just cant do

from folder b file 32: 6 min 54 sec

fuck
man

didnt know recorder was working.

cemetery miss you 117

THE PUBLISHERS

There is an informative article on Proverse by Verner Bickley in the November 2011 number of the online literary magazine, *Asian Cha*, at: www.asiancha.com/content/view/1010/318/

THE INTERNATIONAL PROVERSE PRIZE

The Proverse Prize, an annual international competition for an unpublished single-author book-length work of fiction, non-fiction, or poetry, the original work of the entrant, submitted in English (translations are welcome) was established in January 2008. It is open to all who are at least eighteen on the date they sign the entry form and without restriction of nationality, residence or citizenship.

Founded by Gillian and Verner Bickley, the objectives of the prize are: to encourage excellence and / or excellence and usefulness in publishable written work in the English Language, which can, in varying degrees, "delight and instruct". Entries are invited from anywhere in the world.

The Prize
1) Publication by Proverse Hong Kong, with
2) Cash prize of HKD10,000 (HKD7.80 = approx. USD1.00)

Extent of the Manuscript: within the range of what is usual for the genre of the work submitted.

Annual Entry Deadlines (subject to confirmation and/or change)

Receipt of Entry Fees / Entry Forms begins	[no later than 14 April]
Deadline for receipt of Entry Fees / Entry Forms	31 May
Receipt of entered manuscripts begins	1 May
Deadline for receipt of entered manuscripts	30 June

More information, updated from time to time, is available on the Proverse website: proversepublishing.com

AUTOBIOGRAPHY, MEMOIRS, DIARIES, ETC. PUBLISHED BY PROVERSE HONG KONG

Having read, *cemetery miss you*, may also enjoy the following, published by Proverse.

Bao Bao's Odyssey: From Mao's Shanghai to Capitalist Hong Kong. By Paul Ting. 2012.

The Chinese of Macau a decade after the handover. By Jean Berlie. 2012. Foreword by Geoffrey C. Gunn.

Chocolate's brown study in the bag. By Rupert Kwan Yun Chan. 2011.

The complete court cases of Magistrate Frederick Stewart as reported in *The China Mail*, **July 1881 to March 1882.** Edited with commentary and chapters by Gillian Bickley. Essay by Dr Ian Grant. Preface by The Hon. Mr Justice Bokhary PJ, Court of Final Appeal. 2008. CD. Supported by the Council of the Lord Wilson Heritage Trust.

The development of education in Hong Kong, 1841-1897: as revealed by the early Education Reports of the Hong Kong Government, 1848-1896. Ed. Gillian Bickley. 2002. Hbk. Supported by the Council of the Lord Wilson Heritage Trust.

The Diplomat of Kashgar: A Very Special Agent: The Life of Sir George Macartney, 18 January 1867-19 May 1945. By James McCarthy. 2014. Preface by Graham Leicester, HM Diplomatic Service, 1984-1995.

Gin's tonic: ocean voyage, inner journey. By Virginia MacRobert. 2010. Preface by Ed Vaughan. Supported by Hong Kong Arts Development Council.

The Day They Came. By Gérard Breissan. 2012.

The Golden Needle: the biography of Frederick Stewart (1836-1889). By Gillian Bickley. 1997. Foreword by Lady Saltoun. Introduction by Sir David Wilson (now Lord Wilson). Supported by David C. Lam Institute for East-West Studies, Hong Kong Baptist University.

The Golden Needle: the biography of Frederick Stewart (1836-1889). By Gillian Bickley. Full audio version on 14 CDs. Read by Verner Bickley. Supported by CED, Hong Kong Baptist University.

In Time of War. By Lt. Cmdr. Henry C.S. Collingwood-Selby, R.N. (1898-1992). Ed. Richard Collingwood-Selby (Chile) and Gillian Bickley (Hong Kong). 2013. Supported by the Council of the Lord Wilson Heritage Trust.

A magistrate's court in nineteenth century Hong Kong: Court in Time. Ed. Gillian Bickley. Contributors: Garry Tallentire, Geoffrey Roper, Timothy Hamlett, Christopher Coghlan, Verner Bickley. Preface by Sir T. L. Yang. 1st edn. 2005.

A magistrate's court in 19th century Hong Kong, with additional discussion of "The Opium Ordinance": Court in Time. 2nd edn. 2009.

Memoirs of an Ice-Cream Lady. By Emily Ho. 2011.

Mila the Magician. By Catherine Chin. 2014.

The Misted Mirror. By Gillian Jones. 2011.

A personal journey through sketching: the sketcher's art. By Errol Patrick Hugh. 2009. Introduction by Li Shiqiao. Hbk.

refrain. By Jason S Polley. 2011.

Semper fi! The story of a vietnam era marine. By Orville Leverne Clubb. 2012.

A Shimmering Sea: Hong Kong Stories. By Sophronia Liu. 2012.

Steps to Paradise and beyond: Hawii to China, Saudi Arabia, Hong Kong and Elsewhere. By Verner Bickley. 2013. Preface by Charles E. Morrison, President, East-West Center.

Tightrope! – A Bohemian Tale. By Olga Walló. 2010.

To Eastern Lands: Reflections in prose, photographs and verse of a journey from Melbourne to Bombay, Beijing, and other exotic destinations. By Roger Uren. 2013.

Wannabe backpackers: the Latin American & Kenyan journey of five spoiled teenagers. By Gerald Yeung. 2009.

PLEASE WRITE TO US!

We are interested to read your comments on
cemetery miss you.
Write to our email address, proverse@netvigator.com,
giving us a few sentences which you are willing for us to
publish,
describing your response to this book.
If your comments are chosen to be included
in our E-Newsletter or website,
we will select another title published by Proverse
and send you a complimentary copy.
Please include your name, email address and mailing
address when you write to us, and state whether or not we
may cut or edit your comments for publication.
We will use your initials to attribute your comments.

FIND OUT MORE ABOUT OUR AUTHORS
BOOKS AND EVENTS AND THE PROVERSE PRIZE

Visit our website
http://www.proversepublishing.com

Visit our distributor's website
<www.chineseupress.com>

Follow us on Twitter
Follow news and conversation: <twitter.com/Proversebooks>
OR
Copy and paste the following to your browser window and
follow the instructions: https://twitter.com/#!/ProverseBooks

"Like" us on www.facebook.com/ProversePress

Request our E-Newsletter
Send your request to info@proversepublishing.com.

Availability
Most titles are available in Hong Kong and world-wide
from our Hong Kong based Distributor,
The Chinese University Press of Hong Kong,
The Chinese University of Hong Kong, Shatin, NT,
Hong Kong SAR, China. Web: chineseupress.com

All titles are available from Proverse Hong Kong
and the Proverse Hong Kong UK-based Distributor.

We have stock-holding retailers in Hong Kong,
Singapore (Select Books),
Canada (Elizabeth Campbell Books),
Principality of Andorra (Llibreria La Puça, La Llibreria).

Orders can be made from bookshops in the UK and elsewhere.

Ebooks
Most of our titles are available also as Ebooks.